Memory Man by David Baldacci - Reviewed

By
Anthony Granger

CONTENTS

1. About the Author:

David Baldacci is an American best-selling author. He was born and raised in Richmond, Virginia, and graduated from Virginia Commonwealth University. He went on to receive a law degree from the University of Virginia. He used his law degree to practice law for nine years in Washington, D.C. Baldacci wrote his first book, *Absolute Power*, while he was practicing law. Although he was an avid reader and loved to write stories from childhood onward, it took him over three years to pen his debut work. He wrote on the side for twenty years before he was finally able to write something publishable in 1996. Since then, he has published 29 different novels for adults, and four novels for young readers.

Baldacci and his wife, Michelle, live in Vienna, Virginia, with their two teenage children. Baldacci is the brother of author Sharon Baldacci. Sharon Baldacci was diagnosed with Multiple Sclerosis, which sparked a love for organizations focused on the cure. Baldacci and his wife are the co-founders of the Wish You Well organization, which works to combat illiteracy in the United States.

In addition to his novels, Baldacci has had some of his work turn into film. His novel "Wish You Well" was turned into a film in Virginia recently, and TNT aired a special television series based on his books "King and Maxwell".

Baldacci is known for writing novels that incorporate law, mystery, and crime. While he has written dozens of books, he often recycles and reuses characters, creating series that use the same characters. "The Memory Man", Baldacci's latest work, is the first in the Amos Decker series of novels. He has also created quite a few standalone novels.

2. Themes:

The two most prominent themes in "The Memory Man" are revenge and justice. The killer is obsessed with the idea of revenge, and seeks it on everyone within her path. She is angry not only at her situation, but at her parents for being bribed to stay quiet about her rape, and at those who have raped her. While she does murder both her parents and one of the men that raped her, she seeks her revenge in other ways as well. She chooses symbolism as she murders, focusing all of her murders on someone who is somehow tied to Decker. While the things done against her were incredibly brutal, the killer goes many steps further than what would simply be fair, and plans a retribution that is inexplicably worse than the original crimes.

The other main theme of the novel is justice, which the entire town of Burlington and the police force are focused on. Decker is unable to stop looking for justice for his murdered family, and it is his quest for justice that causes him to have such a hard time living his life. When the school shootings happen, the entire town is preoccupied with bringing the killer to justice, as well. However, as the police investigate the murders more closely, Decker finds that the killer has been seeking her own justice through revenge. Both parties get the justice they so crave, as the killer finishes her revenge and gets justice on those that hurt her, and the police force and Decker find and kill the murderers from Burlington.

3. Symbols:

The most prevalent symbol in "The Memory Man" is Decker's association with colors. His synesthesia means that he sees people and events in colors, and each color has a specific feeling or meaning associated to it. For instance, he sees Leopold in the color yellow, which he often knows to mean that the person is mean or calculating. His family's murders are seen in the color blue, and when sadness or death occurs, blue covers the event. Lastly, Belinda/Billy is seen in the color 'grey', homage to her own confusion. Grey, a color that exists between black and white, mirrors Belinda's cross between male and female.

In addition to colors, Decker is also infiltrated by numbers. When he is about to undergo a hard situation or a devastating event is about to take place, he sees the number three marching toward him mercilessly. The number three is a symbol of impending danger.

4. Settings:

Burlington is a small town where most of the residents are poor. Foreclosures are numerous around the town, and most people are working dead-end jobs. It used to be a military base, but has since closed down. There is nothing particularly exciting about the town of Burlington, and it gets few visitors. As a result, it is more convincing that the murders were related to Decker than it would have been had the book been set in a more exciting city.

5. Short Summary:

Amos Decker's wife and young daughter were murdered brutally. A year and a half later, Decker's life has fallen apart. He has left his job on the police force and has lost his house. He is homeless, but after catching a glimpse of himself in the mirror, he is ashamed and knows that his wife and daughter would have been too.

He starts taking freelance investigative work when his old partner from the police force informs him that they've made an arrest in the murder case of his family. Decker finds out that the man, Sebastian Leopold, turned himself in. Decker arrives at the police station and impersonates a lawyer in order to interview Leopold. Leopold claims that he murdered Decker's family because Decker dissed him at the 7-Eleven. Decker does not remember him, and Leopold doesn't recognize him when he comes in.

Decker, an ex-football player, suffered a massive hit during a college football game that caused him to die and come back to life twice. Through the brain trauma, he developed synesthesia and hyperthymesia because his brain was rewired. He is now unable to forget anything that has happened to him since the accident, and his brain crosses senses. He sees his neighborhood in the color blue after his family's murders, and the number three pops up when danger is imminent. His condition also makes him an excellent detective, as details are not lost on him.

As he begins to get off the street, there's a school shooting at the local high school and Decker is asked to help with the investigation. Decker shows up at the scene of the crime and begins to place together the killer's steps. He finds that the killer had access to the school through an underground bomb shelter he was told about by a senior at the school he was seeing. He and his ex-partner, Lancaster, look throughout the school for clues. They find that the killer has taken all of Decker's football trophies, and hidden different things in a bomb shelter underground. Decker is convinced that the killer must have picked the school in an effort to target him for some reason, though he still doesn't understand why.

It becomes obvious that the killer has targeted the high school because of Decker, but the connection is unclear. As Decker and the police force investigate more, they find that the killer is also connected to Leopold. Leopold did not actually murder Decker's family as he was in jail in a neighboring city at the time. He also could not have murdered the students at the school, as he was in police custody.

A ballistics test, however, shows that the gun used to murder Decker's family was also used in the school shooting. Decker is convinced that Leopold and the killer are working together, but he still is unsure who the killer is and why he is being targeted. Decker uses his own personal need to bring his family justice to spur him into finding the killer of the high school students.

One of the agents that Decker is working with is murdered, and the killer once again leaves notes for Decker. This addition to the story causes a local reporter, Alexandra Jamison, to contact Decker. She wants to get a story, but Decker is rude and unwilling to give her one. As the details of the investigation come out, Decker realizes that he misunderstood the killer's first clue about why he is murdering. He realizes that the killer is someone he knew from his time spent at a research institute twenty years earlier, though he still doesn't know which person it is. He and a reporter that he has befriended go to the research institute's old site in an effort to find out more information. The institute, however, has moved. They find a local florist who gives them the information for one of the doctors who used to work at the institute but has since retired.

While there, they meet with the former doctor and inform him that they believe the killer is from the institute and is seeking retribution on Decker. While the doctor can't recall a patient who had a problem with Decker, he and Decker do agree that there was a psychologist who disliked him. Decker believes the psychologist may be the murderer. They get his information from the doctor and head to his house. They find that one of the research psychologists has also been killed.

They return to Burlington in an effort to understand more about the killer. When they get there, they realize that Decker has seen the killer before, when she was waitressing at a local bar. They ask the bartender about her and find out that the waitress was actually a woman in drag. They look at the footage from the bar that night, and Decker realizes that the bartender was correct. He remembers a patient at the institute who had problems with her sexuality, and wonders if it could be her.

The agents, Decker, and the reporter fly back to the institute and ask to speak to one of the doctors who is still working there. The doctor confirms that a patient, Belinda Wyatt, was a hermaphrodite when she was in the institute and struggled deeply with her sexuality. Decker realizes that Belinda Wyatt must be the killer.

They investigate Belinda's past and find that her parents were paid off to keep quiet about her brutal gang-rape, and that Belinda has murdered them in revenge. She had been raped by a police officer, members of the football team, the football coach, and an assistant principal. Each of the murders at the school were done as a symbolic attempt to exact revenge on those that raped her.

They speak to the father of one of the rapists, and he confirms that he paid off Belinda's parents to keep quiet. When the investigators arrive at the Wyatt's house, they find their bodies as well as some letters Belinda had written that hint toward the future murders. However, they are still unaware of how Leopold and Belinda know each other.

They call the father of the rapist again, and find that he has been given an article in the mail about an organization called Justice Denied, which targets police officers who have committed heinous crimes and not been charged. When the trio looks up the members of Justice Denied, they find Leopold's name on the list following the murder of his wife and daughter.

They realize that Leopold and Wyatt know each other through this organization. Decker realizes that Wyatt feels personally slighted by Decker's decision to become a police officer after being a football player, both of which are positions that took advantage of her.

Decker goes on the website and ends up connecting with Leopold and Wyatt. He offers himself up in order to save others from potential murders. They send him on a goose chase to make sure that he comes alone, and then kidnap him and drive him to a secluded area. While there, he is able to convince Belinda that Leopold is a con-man who murdered his own family and gets sadistic pleasure out of watching others in pain. Leopold shoots Belinda out of fear now that she knows the truth, and Decker suffocates him. Decker escapes and goes to call the police, and the murder mysteries are solved.

One of the FBI agents Decker worked with invites him to join the FBI. He also invites the reporter that Decker solved the case with. The two agree to move to Washington DC and take the jobs offered them.

6. Chapters 1-3

What Happens:

Amos Decker is a police investigator who arrives home late one night to find his brother-in-law, Johnny, his wife, Cassie, and his daughter, Molly murdered. Johnny's throat has been slit as he sat drinking at the table, Cassie has been mutilated and shot in the forehead, and Molly was strangled. Amos believes there is nothing left for him to live for, and contemplates taking his own life by putting a pistol in his mouth. He calls 911, however, and the police arrive and talk him out of it. He sees the color blue in the house everywhere.

Fifteen months later, Decker's grief has overcome him. He was forced to quit the police force as a result, and his house got foreclosed on because of his lack of income. Eventually, he began living in a box outside of the homeless shelter. He has also gained a lot of weight. He remembers his stint as a pro football player, where he was tackled and died twice on the field, but was brought back to life.

At that point, he developed a brain condition that keeps him from forgetting details. He realizes that his family would be ashamed of how he's turned out, so he gets a job as a private investigator and moves into a motel. Decker goes to a bar to trail the couple he's been hired to follow. The couple is a con-artist and a much-younger woman with access to her father's money. Decker approaches the man to blackmail him and records the conversation. He gives the man a one-way ticket to leave town.

Analysis:

It is obvious from the first page that Amos Decker's life has not gone the way he envisioned it. His grief over the loss of his family has caused him to spiral into depression. On top of the natural grief that the murders have brought on his life, Decker's synesthesia and hyperthymesia make it impossible for him to forget any of the details of the murder, making the grief even deeper than it had been before. He sees people more as numbers and colors, rather than for who they are. This ability enables him to compartmentalize and remain unattached to the people he meets and investigates.

Important Terms/Characters:
Amos Decker – a police investigator whose family was murdered a year and a half earlier; he now has synesthesia and an above-average memory.
Cassandra Decker – Amos's wife, a murder victim
Molly Decker – Amos's 9 year old daughter, a murder victim
Johnny Sacks – Amos's brother-in-law, a murder victim
Residence Inn – the motel where Amos lives after he gets off the street
Slick – a con-man that Amos Decker is hired to bust
Jenny Marks -   the woman that Slick is seeing, who is rich off Daddy's money.
Hyperthymesia – a condition Decker has where a person's memory is exceptional and has no faults
Synesthesia – a condition Decker has where two senses are connected

Study Questions:
   1. How do Decker's hyperthymesia and synesthesia intensify his grief and depression?

Interesting Quotes:
"I'm not normal. I haven't been normal since I stepped on that field and took that hit."

7. Chapters 4-6

What Happens:

Decker is having breakfast in the dining room of the hotel when his old partner, Mary Lancaster, comes in. He doesn't want her to join him, but she does anyway. She reluctantly tells them, even though she's not allowed to, that they've made an arrest in the murder case of his wife and daughter. Lancaster tells him that a man named Sebastian Leopold has turned himself in for the murder of all three of his family members.

She tells Decker that Leopold murdered his family because he was mad that Decker dissed him at the 7-eleven. Decker doesn't remember him. Decker wants to meet Leopold, but Lancaster tells him he needs to back off and not interfere with the investigation, since he isn't on the police force. Decker continues to think about the way his brain functions differently.

He reveals that his brain changed after being hit on the football field by Dwayne LeCroix. He gets a phone call from a reporter, Alexandra Jamison, who wants more information on Leopold's arrest. He hangs up on her and heads to his old precinct to meet Leopold.

Analysis:

Decker showcases his inability to connect to others with his reaction to Lancaster. His lack of emotional response to her presence, and his rudeness when she tells him about the arrest, both show that he has a difficult time connecting to others. The arrest of Leopold seems fishy, since he turned himself in. In addition, Lancaster's comment that the murder occurred because Decker "dissed" the murder at the 7-11 doesn't seem to stand up, as Decker doesn't remember it and his memory is flawless.

Important Terms/Characters:

Mary Lancaster –Decker's old partner, who is still a member of the police force
Sebastian Leopold – the man who turned himself in for the murders of three of Decker's family
Dwayne LeCroix – a football player who hit Decker so hard he had a brain injury
Alexandra Jamison – a reporter who wants to interview Decker
7 – Eleven – the place where Leopold apparently met Decker which caused him to want to murder the family

Study Questions:
1. What prompted Lancaster to tell Decker about Sebastian Leopold? What risk did she take in doing so?

Interesting Quotes:

"He had woken up this morning with not a single purpose in life, other than to live until the next morning. Now that had all changed."

8. Chapters 7-9

What Happens:

When Decker arrives at the precinct, squad cars are pulling out rapidly and the SWAT team is rushing out of the parking lot. Decker asks an old friend and current police officer, Pete Rourke, where they are going. He informs him there's been a shooting at the local high school. Decker realizes the precinct will be empty, so he decides to go in. He goes to a store across the street and buys a lot of fancy clothes to clean up his appearance.

He tells the lady at the front desk that Leopold will need an attorney, pretending to be one. The lady at the front desk calls Sally Brimmer to come meet him. He informs her that Leopold will need a lawyer, lying to her. He hands her someone else's card and she assumes he is actually a lawyer and leads him to Leopold's cell even though it's against her better judgment.

When Decker gets to Leopold's cell, Leopold doesn't recognize him even though Leopold had said he murdered his family because he snubbed him at the 7-eleven. Leopold questions him about the murders, as a lawyer would, and Leopold leaves out key details. Decker is about to leave when he hears a lot of footsteps coming toward the cell. He escapes and takes the bus back to his hotel, but when he gets there, there are cop cars outside of his room.

Analysis:

Decker showcases his need to take matters into his own hands in this chapter. He doesn't heed the warning from Lancaster not to get involved, and instead, uses his intelligence and his knowledge of the precinct to weasel his way into the investigation. Even more interesting, Leopold doesn't recognize him when he enters the holding cell.

That, in addition to the missing and incorrect details about the murders, places suspicion on Leopold that he wasn't the one who actually murdered Decker's family. The reader is left trying to figure out what happened. It is obvious that Decker, while talented, does not know where the boundaries are in his own life when he tries to interfere with the investigation. He also doesn't care who else gets in trouble for his actions.

Important Terms/Characters:

Sally Brimmer – a woman at the police precinct who shows Decker to Leopold's cell
Pete Rourke – a man on the police force
Mansfield High – the high school where there was a shooting

Study Questions:
9. What does Leopold do or say that makes Decker suspicious of his story that he murdered his family?
10. What does Decker do to overstep professional boundaries?

11. Chapters 10-11

What Happens:

When Decker gets to his hotel, a few police officers and the captain of the squad are waiting for him, along with Sally Brimmer, the woman he lied to in order to get to Leopold's jail cell. When Captain Miller gets onto Decker about lying to her, he manipulates the situation by making it seem like Brimmer made messed up since she didn't ask enough questions and assumed things. Miller tells him not to poke his nose into the murder case anymore, but asks him about what he learned from his conversation with Leopold.

Decker tells him that Leopold is not the real killer because there were too many flaws in his story. Captain Miller agrees, but thinks that they should let justice run the course. Decker goes down to Mansfield High, which is swarming with cops and parents. He sits on the stadium bleachers and tries to figure out how the shooter got in, and also how he managed to flee the scene without being caught. Lancaster finds Decker sitting on the bleacher. She tells him that she knows about his conversation with Leopold, and that Miller wants to hire him to help investigate the school shooting. She asks him if he would like to come see the Mansfield crime scene with her.

Analysis:

Decker's obsession with his own case shows that he is still grieving and having a hard time coming to grips with his family's murders. He is unable to see where he is wrong or overstepping. However, it is obvious that he is and was a good private investigator, as even the police captain wants him to work on the Mansfield High shooting. The reader must get the feeling that the two events are connected in some way or another, however, with

Leopold being in jail during the time of the shooting, it only makes his story more iffy.

Important Terms/Characters:

Captain Mackenzie Miller – the captain of the police force who shows up at Decker's hotel

Study Questions:
1. How did Decker trick Sally Brimmer?
2. What new job does Decker receive as a result of the Mansfield school shooting?

12. Chapters 12-14

What Happens:

Lancaster takes Decker to the body of the first victim, a senior girl named Debbie Watson who was killed while at her locker. They walk from body to body, and Lancaster puts together an idea of the order that the shooter took when on his killing spree. She tells Decker that the killer was dressed in full camo and his face was completely covered, but he was a big man. Decker can't figure out how the man escaped the school. He is worried that the man has been evacuated with the other students, or is still hiding in the building.

Decker spends the night searching the building, and ends up in the library with Lancaster poring over witness reports. He finds one from Melissa Dalton, who heard a loud vacuum sound and a door open an hour before school started, and over an hour before the shooting started.

Decker goes into the cafeteria and finds the large, walk-in freezer. He opens the door to test the sound, finding it's the same one Melissa Dalton heard. He also finds that the temperature of the freezer has been turned up to 45 degrees, allowing the shooter to hide inside. He finds another place for the shooter to hide weapons and a possible escape route.

Analysis:
Decker's brilliant mind comes into play in this chapter, as he is able to remember details from witness testimonies that others may not. His memory is what allows him to figure out that the shooter was in the cafeteria freezer, leading the police force to find the holding space for the weapons. His keen detective skills also allow him to piece together how the shooter may have accomplished the task he set out for.

Important Terms/Characters:

Debbie Watson – the first person to be murdered in the school shooting, a high school senior
Melissa Dalton – a student who gave a testimony about a loud vacuum sound an hour before the shooting began

Study Questions:
1. Describe the shooter. What did he look like?
2. Why is Decker concerned that they haven't caught the shooter?

13. Chapter 15-17

What Happens:
When Decker leaves without saying a word to trace his own theory, Lancaster expresses her annoyance and acknowledges that this isn't the first time he's done so. He is often leaving a room and tracking his own theories without communicating to anyone. Decker expresses some doubts about his involvement in the case, but Lancaster quickly tells him that he must participate because they need him. They wonder if perhaps the victims were shot in a different order than previously believed.

When Lancaster heads home to take a quick nap, Decker heads to the courthouse for Sebastian Leopold's arraignment. Captain Miller and Lancaster go to the arraignment to support Decker. The judge finds out that Leopold has refused legal counsel, even a public defender and is mad at the prosecuting attorney. He reschedules the arraignment for the next day so that an attorney can be given to the defendant because if he doesn't have one, the case is likely to be thrown out. Alexandra Jamison is in attendance and wants to get a quote from Decker after the arraignment, but Decker refuses to speak to her.

Analysis:
Once again, Decker's emotional deficiencies are on the forefront as he simply walks out of the room without the courtesy of telling Lancaster where he is going. This trait, along with others, is a direct result of his brain trauma and shows how he has changed over the course of his life. However, even with these deficiencies, it is obvious that Decker has a good support system, as both Captain Miller and Lancaster show up at Leopold's arraignment to support him. Leopold's refusal to get a lawyer is suspicious at this point.

Important Terms/Characters:

Sheila Lynch – the prosecuting attorney for the case against
Sebastian Leopold

Study Questions:
1. What does the arraignment tell the reader about Decker?
   About Leopold?
2. What role does Alexandra Jamison play in Decker's life at
   this point?

14. Chapters 18-19

What Happens:
Decker leaves the arraignment and heads to his home. It is still vacant because nobody wants to purchase it after the triple homicides. As he goes through his neighborhood, he is surrounded by the color blue, the same color he saw the night his family was murdered. The color has extended past his own house and out across the neighborhood as well. When he goes into Molly's room, he finds a note on the wall of the bedroom that is addressed to him from the murderer. The murderer refers to him as a "brother". He calls Lancaster over to the house immediately.

Lancaster and Miller arrive at the scene with a forensics team, and Miller questions how the murderer would have known Decker would come back to the house. Decker admits he'd been there before.

He leaves and walks over to the 7-Eleven, where Leopold said he was dissed. He shows Leopold's picture to a woman behind the counter and an employee named Billy, but neither of them recognize Leopold. Lancaster calls him and informs him that they've done a ballistics test on the gun at the high school and it was the same gun that the murderer used to kill Decker's wife, Cassie.

Analysis:
Once again, Decker's obsession with finding out who is behind his family's murders leads him to abandon social cues. It is obvious the murderer is following him and that the murders are personal in nature, since the murderer left a note on his daughter's bedroom wall. However, with Leopold in custody, it adds to the mystery of who is beyond the murders.

In addition, the newfound knowledge that the murderer at the high school is the same as the murderer who killed his family adds further confusion to the plot. There seems to be no link between the high school and Decker, however, there is for the murderer. In addition, Leopold's imprisonment during the time of the shooting hints that he is not actually the murderer.

Important Terms/Characters:
Billy – an employee at the 7-Eleven

Study Questions:
1. What do you learn about the murderer in these chapters? How is this information important?
2. What is the significance of the color blue to Amos Decker?

Interesting Quotes:
"As his large feet carried him down the sidewalk, the color blue intensified in his head until it seemed that the entire world had been covered in it. Even the sun seemed to have been transformed into an enormous blueberry so utterly swollen that it seemed it might burst at any moment."

"We are so much alike, Amos. So much. Like brothers. Do you have a brother? Of course you don't. I checked. Sisters, yes, but no brother. So can I be yours? We're really all the other has now. We need each other."

15. Chapters 20-22

What Happens:
Decker returns to Mansfield High now that he has the information that the murders of his family are connected to the school shooting. He believes that the murderer is the same, thus clearing Leopold since he was in jail at the time of the school shootings. He reads through the accounts and finds a discrepancy of about five minutes between when Debbie was shot and when she asked to leave class. He goes to her locker (the location where she was shot) and rifles through it, finding a notebook with a drawing of a man in camo with a heart next to it. Decker and Lancaster decide to interview Debbie's parents, George and Beth Watson.

They ask if they recognize the man in the drawing or know any information about an older man Debbie was dating. Beth says she suspected Debbie was dating someone, but neither of them know. Decker and Lancaster search Debbie's room. Decker notices a musical score on a chalkboard in her bedroom and believes it was a message from the shooter because it's written with a left hand, not a right, like Debbie would write.

Decker and Lancaster find out that George and Beth were out of town and left Debbie alone, which seems to be when the man came over. They try to figure out if Debbie helped plan the school shooting or not. Decker begins to see the number three. He finds out that Debbie's grandfather worked on the army base near the school when he was alive. Lancaster finds out that Debbie's chalkboard was indeed a message for Decker from the shooter.

Analysis:
Debbie Watson proves to be an interesting character, as she is now a suspect in the school shooting as well. Her relationship with the man in camo is suspect, however, her death also makes it seem obvious that if she was part of the shooting plan, it did not go as she expected. Her parents, brokenhearted over the death of their

daughter, are unable to accept that she might have had anything to do with the shooting, or the shooter himself. Decker's emotional deficiencies are put on display yet again as he is unable to relate to her parents, even as he's gone through something similar.

Important Terms/Characters:
George Watson – Debbie's father
Beth Watson – Debbie's mother
Simon Watson – George's grandfather, who worked at the army base before he passed away

Study Questions:
1. What is the significance in the difference of time between Debbie's shooting and her release from class? Why is this detail important? Why does it cause Decker to become suspicious?
2. What is the importance of Debbie's chalkboard? What does it tell the reader about the shooter?

Interesting Quotes:
"There could be no commiseration among such people despite the seeming commonality of loss, because it was actually each parent's totally unique hell."

16. Chapters 23-25

What Happens:
Decker reveals that those at the research institute called him an "acquired savant" after his football injury. He arrives at the courthouse for the arraignment, and finds that Leopold now has a public defender. The lawyer claims that Leopold was off his bipolar medication when he confessed and that he did not commit the murders. He was in jail in a town close by at the time of the murders.

The prosecuting attorney is shocked to hear that, but the judge scolds her for not doing thorough enough research. Leopold is let go, and although Alex Jamison tries to interview Decker, he refuses. He follows Leopold to a bar on the other side of the town and observes him. Then he goes and sits next to him and tries to strike up a conversation about why Leopold admitted to the murders. Leopold gets up and leaves.

Decker waits for a little bit before he decides to follow him, but when he goes outside, Leopold is gone. He searches for Leopold but doesn't find anything. He goes back to the high school and tells Lancaster about Leopold's release. An FBI Agent Bogart shows up at the scene and wants to speak with Decker. Decker tells him what he knows about the events of the shootings. While Decker recognizes that Leopold did not commit the murders because his alibis are sufficient, he doesn't trust him and tells Bogart that he is a dangerous man.

Analysis:
Decker continues to find Leopold suspect, even when his alibis point against his guilt in the murders. His curiosity causes him to follow Leopold to a shady bar, where he questions him. Once again, Decker puts himself in harm's way and shows a lack of regard for his own well-being. Leopold's behaviors flit between lucid and strange, and both the reader and Decker have a hard time

gauging if Leopold is out of it or if he's lucid. Adding to his mystique, Leopold disappears within seconds of leaving the bar.

Important Terms/Characters:
Special Agent Ross Bogart – An FBI agent sent from Washington DC to help investigate the school shooting
Special Agent Lafferty – Ross Bogart's assistant who takes notes

Study Questions:
1. Describe Leopold's behaviors and mannerisms. How do they further Decker's belief that he is dangerous and suspicious?
2. Do you believe Leopold's alibis? Why or why not?

Interesting Quotes:
"A squatter for life is inhabiting my mind. And he happens to be me."

17. Chapters 26-28

What Happens:
As Decker retraces the shooter's route in the high school, he recalls that the school was built in 1946, just before the start of the Cold War. He wonders if there is a secret passageway or underground bomb shelter located in the school. They go back to the Watsons' house to ask for confirmation. George is drunk and depressed because his wife is leaving him.

Beth is also drunk but is more in control of her faculties. She confirms that George's grandfather had told her that there was an underground bomb shelter from the Cold War era. Decker calls the US Army to see if they can provide him with more information, but he is out of luck. They head back to the school cafeteria to look for a place that could lead into the bomb shelter. They find a part of the wall that opens and heads down to the shelter.

When they climb down, they find that someone has been tampering with the shelter very recently. They continue to explore and find that the shelter leads into the shop class, as well. Decker believes that Debbie and the shooter had met in the shop class, where he had knocked her unconscious and then dragged her to her locker and killed her. Decker is confused by the size of a shoeprint that doesn't match a tall, burly man like the shooter, the amount of space in the opening that the shooter would have to get through.

Analysis:
It is obvious that whoever the shooter at the high school is, he or she has a lot of experience and knowledge of the area. The connection of the base and the knowledge to go after Debbie Watson for information showcases a man who knows how to manipulate a young girl and a situation. Decker's training and his mind being a steel trap help him recall information essential for his police training. Decker's life has been changed rapidly in two different ways: the hit when he was in college, and the murder of

his family. In the same way that his life changed rapidly and without warning, the shooter is able to manipulate and change things without warning as well.

Important Terms/Characters:
McDonald Army Base – the army base that is shut down but located near the school

Study Questions:
1. What is significant about the shoe size of the prints in the bomb shelter?
2. Why is it important to note that the school was opened shortly before the Cold War?

18. Chapter 29-31

What Happens:
Decker discovers that the killer escaped through another wall in the shelter that leads out to the military base next door. Bogart finds Decker's mind extraordinary and suspicious, but recognizes that he is an asset to the case because of it. Decker and Lancaster agree to Bogart's request that they let the FBI in on any future discoveries they come across with the shooting. Decker awakes to a scraping sound outside of his hotel room, and finds the body of Special Agent Lafferty outside.

She has multiple stab wounds in her heart and similar wounds to his late wife. He looks for the killer but cannot find him. Decker asks Bogart about Lafferty's plans for that evening and finds that she had run to a local pharmacy since she'd forgotten some items at home. They get the camera footage from the pharmacy, but cannot see the killer's face as he abducts her into the alley. Decker believes the killer may have been in uniform in order to trick Lafferty into trusting him.

Decker goes back to the 7-Eleven and sees the newspaper has his meeting with Leopold on the front page, courtesy of Alex Jamison. She shows up at his hotel in an effort to force him to talk about the real story instead of the one she made up, but Decker warns her she should go away or the shooter may kill her next.

Analysis:
Another murder has occurred, once again, linked to Decker in a non-obvious way. Decker's concerns that anyone close to him further exacerbate the problem. As he tries to convince Jamison not to work with him in an effort to protect her, he is unknowingly isolating himself from a support system. The reader has to wonder if this is part of the killer's plan, to isolate him in order to get to him.

Important Terms/Characters:
N/A

Study Questions:
1. How is Agent Lafferty's death related to Decker? Is it symbolic of anything?
2. Why does Decker believe the killer may have been impersonating an officer?

19. Chapters 32-34

What Happens:
Decker believes that the killer is giving Jamison her tips. When they go to the morgue to identify the body of Lafferty, they find she was given a sedative that made her incapable of fighting back against her abductor. There is a note carved on her backside with a knife that is directed at Decker. Bogart is grieved by Lafferty's death and attempts to physically harm Decker, who pins him to the ground.

When Decker and Bogart calm down, they try to find the link between Decker and the killer, as well as the killer and Leopold. Decker goes back to the bar where he talked to Leopold and asks the bartender about him. He notices that the waitress that was working there that night is no longer there, and the bartender alludes to the fact that she may have been a man in drag, but she disappeared that night. Decker believes this person is the one who leaked photos to Jamison and provided Leopold with the getaway. Lancaster sends out the forensics team and a sketch artist to try and uncover more information.

Analysis:
Decker's conversation with the bartender proves to be enlightening, as he is beginning to realize that the waitress is an important key in the puzzle of murders. While Decker doesn't know how the waitress is involved, the bartender's comment that the waitress may be a man in drag points to doubts that the shooter was actually a man in the first place. The investigation into the murderer is now wide-open, as the physical descriptions of the shooter may be more fluid than once believed.

Important Terms/Characters:
N/A

Study Questions:

1. How does the bartender help further the investigation? What information does the bartender have that allows Decker and the police force to re-evaluate their previous beliefs?

Interesting Quotes:
"When the will was there, anything was possible. And it seemed anything had been possible here."

20. Chapters 35-37

What Happens:
Decker goes back to the school's bomb shelter to search for clues. While there, he finds football padding in a heap and realizes that the shooter pretended to be larger than he/she was by wearing football padding. Further investigation finds that his trophies in the school are missing, making it obvious that the school shooting was a personal vendetta against Decker.

The FBI finds the uniform of a police officer in the alley where he was killed, and the name on the uniform is Decker's. Decker goes to his storage unit to look for his uniform, but finds it missing. Bogart shows up at the scene and allows Decker to look over the uniform that was used. While he's looking, Decker finds that the length of the hem has been brought up and the shirt has been taken in so a smaller person could fit inside of it.

Decker returns to his hotel to find it littered with items and notes calling him a child killer. Jamison arrives at the hotel to apologize to him. The two agree to work together after Jamison tells him she won't publish anything without his permission.

Analysis:
It is obvious that whoever the shooter is, he or she is very skilled at hiding his/her tracks. It is obvious that the shooter is deliberately sending the police on a wild goose chase, but why? Does the shooter want the police to investigate Decker for the murders? Does the shooter aim to capture Decker for his or herself? It's unclear what the shooter's intentions are, but it is obvious that the shooter is not an amateur.

Important Terms/Characters:
N/A

Study Questions:

1. How has Jamison made Decker's life more difficult than it was previously?
2. Why might the shooter have worn football pads? What benefit did the shooter gain from this decision?

Interesting Quotes:
"So the question becomes, is it someone who's from Burlington who had a grudge against you all these years? Big football star versus some nobody in the background who was jealous of your success? The fact that he took the trophies might indicate it is someone local. Who you went to Mansfield with? He might have thought you were gone for good when you went on to college, and then you come back here and become a cop and do all these great things. And all these years the hatred is building and festering until the guy just explodes."

21. Chapters 38-39

What Happens:
Jamison and Decker go to Decker's storage unit to look through his things. She questions him about his brain injury, and the two discuss his guilt over his family's murders. They believe Decker may have been on a team with the killer at some point. Decker leaves the storage unit abruptly. Decker and Jamison arrive at the police station and meet with Lancaster.

Decker wants Lancaster to read the interview she had with Leopold verbatim because something sounds fishy. When they're reading the interview, Decker realizes that Leopold never said that the 7-Eleven was near his home, and that it is actually part of an address, not the location of a convenience store. Jamison drives Decker to Chicago.

Analysis:
Decker and Jamison's newfound relationship complicates matters, as now Decker has involved yet another person in his saga. His inability to take social cues has transferred over to Jamison, as he leaves her twice without saying a word. However, his brilliant mind is once again on display as he catches a minute detail in Lancaster's interview that changes the course of the investigation.

Once again, the killer proves that he or she wants Decker to follow a rabbit trail, perhaps ensuring that by the time he catches up to them, more deaths will occur. The killer is as straight-forward as can be, even giving Decker the address of when he dissed someone. Decker's memory, although known for its greatness, is put to the test as even with an address he can't seem to recall who he "dissed".

Important Terms/Characters:
Mallard 2000 – the email address of the killer, referring to Duckton Avenue in Chicago

Study Questions:

1. Why did Decker originally believe that he dissed the shooter at a 7-Eleven convenience store? Why did this misunderstanding occur?

Interesting Quotes:

"Just keep me informed, Jamison. And watch him. He's beyond brilliant, but even brilliant people do stupid things."

22. Chapters 40-42

What Happens:
Decker and Jamison travel to Chicago and find the address that the killer left for him. Decker realizes that the address is that of the Cognitive Research Institute, which studied Decker's brain after his accident. When they arrive at the Institute, however, they find that the Cognitive Research Institute is no longer located there.

Decker recognizes a flower shop in the same building, however, and goes inside. He speaks with Daisy, the owner of the flower shop. She tells him that the Institute has since moved locations, but that one of the research doctors still lives in the area. Decker asks for Dr. Rabinowitz's address, and he and Jamison go to visit him. Dr. Rabinowitz is blind. Decker tells him about the school shooting and his belief that the killer may have been a patient at the Institute, but Dr. Rabinowitz finds that hard to believe since he cannot recall a patient who disliked Decker.

Jamison wonders if the killer might have been one of the professionals at the Institute. Decker remembers a psychologist named Chris Sizemore who disliked him due to all of the extra attention he received. While Rabinowitz agrees that Sizemore didn't like Decker, he also doesn't believe Sizemore is capable of murder. However, he agrees to call the Institute to get Sizemore's number and location so Jamison and Decker can do further investigation.

Analysis:
As the case continues to unfold, Decker is being forced to come clean about his memory and the abnormalities of his brain function. The parts of Decker's life that he wanted to keep locked at certain points are now becoming fully known, and he is having to trust others where he normally had to trust himself.

In addition, Jamison's acknowledgement that the killer could be a psychologist or research doctor opens an entirely new angle into the investigation, as previously, Decker had not thought of psychologists or doctors as someone he could have wronged. Dr. Rabinowitz's acknowledgement that Dr. Sizemore left the Institute a few years prior is troublesome, as it seems he may be hiding the reason for Sizemore's departure.

Important Terms/Characters:
Chris Sizemore – a psychologist of the Cognitive Research Institute who disliked Decker
Dr. Rabinowitz – one of the research doctors from the Cognitive Research Institute
Cognitive Research Institute – the research institute where Decker attended after his brain injury
Daisy – the owner of the flower shop in the same building that the Cognitive Research Institute used to be located in

Study Questions:
1. What effect did the Cognitive Research Institute have on Decker? How could it be related to the murders?
2. Who is Chris Sizemore? Dr. Rabinowitz? Are they suspects in the case?

Interesting Quotes:
"Now that you mention it, I do remember Chris having issues with that. Whether it was from a genuine dislike of you, or rather from the effects of his personal issues that later led him to leave the institute, I don't know. But he seemed to think that with you our priorities were off."

23. Chapter 43-45

What Happens:
Jamison and Decker leave Dr. Rabinowitz's house and immediately drive to Sizemore's house in hopes that they will run into him. When they get there, Decker tells Jamison to wait in the car because he doesn't want her to get hurt. He goes inside and finds that the house has been abandoned, and that there are no signs of anyone having lived in it for quite some time.

When he goes upstairs, he finds Sizemore decomposing on the bed and a note scrawled on the wall to Decker, telling him that he is too late. The FBI and police show up at the house and do forensics testing, confirming that the dead man is Sizemore. Decker cannot recall any other person at the Institute who had a problem with him, however. He tries to convince Jamison to leave town for her own safety, but she refuses.

When they return to Mansfield, they meet up with Lancaster. She tells him that she has found that most of the people who died, other than Debbie Watson, were football players. She thinks there must be a link between the killings and the football team. Decker believes he will never remember who he dissed because his memory doesn't fail him.

Analysis:
Sizemore's death throws an entirely new wrench into the investigation. It is obvious now that whoever killed Decker's family and the students at the school knew about the Institute and about his problems with Sizemore. In addition, Decker seems to realize that the stakes are higher than before, as he asks Jamison to leave town in order to protect her. In addition, it seems that whoever the killer is has a problem with football, as many of the victim were football players and Decker's trophies were missing.

There must be a link between football and the killings, and memory and the killings. Decker's memory cannot serve him fast enough, as he finds that he is always one step behind the killer. Nevertheless, Decker feels hopeless as he realizes he will never be able to remember the person who he dissed, as he doesn't forget so there is nothing to remember. This point makes the reader skeptical of Leopold's initial claims that Decker dissed someone and paints the killer as even more suspicious than he or she already is.

Important Terms/Characters:
N/A

Study Questions:
1. What is the link between Sizemore and Decker? How do they know each other?
2. What does Sizemore's death tell you about the killer?

Interesting Quotes:
"Wrong again. If he's rotted now, it took you long enough. Keep trying. Maybe you'll get there. Or maybe not. Xoxo, bro."

24. Chapter 46-48

What Happens:
Decker and Lancaster return to the bar where Decker first met
Leopold to question the bartender for a second time. He asks the
bartender about the waitress in drag, finding out that the waitress
disappeared at the same time that Leopold did. Decker realizes that
the bartender drives a car that makes very little sound, and that the
waitress probably borrowed his car to take Leopold home, then
returned the keys without him seeing.

They find the security footage from the bar for the night he met
Leopold and see the waitress get into the car to pick Leopold up.
While she is very convincing as a woman, Decker thinks it is a
man in disguise. As Lancaster and Decker are headed back to the
station, they find out that there has been a crime at Lancaster's
house. When they get to Lancaster's house, she is hysterical at the
amount of patrol cars around her.

The Captain assures her that none of her family is harmed. When
Decker goes inside, he finds that the killer has made mannequins
of each of Lancaster's family members and done to the
mannequins what he or she had done to Decker's family as a
warning. A threatening message is left in Lancaster's house, and
Decker walks out.

Analysis:
The closer Decker and Lancaster get to solving the crime, the more
obvious the clues are that point to the problem being a personal
one between Decker and someone else. Decker and Lancaster's
trip to the bar and their viewing of the tapes is the first substantial
clue that the killer was the waitress. However, the drag component
of the killer's outfit makes it hard for the police—or the reader—to
make any educated guesses about who the killer could be. Unlike
most crime scenes, half of the population is not eliminated due to
gender.

Lancaster's family's crime scene points to a killer who understands Decker's motivations. While he is not an emotional man or one who is easily attached to others, he has shown a deal of care for Jamison in his effort to get her to leave, and now for Lancaster, as he obviously feels remorse about her family. The killer is also starting to get to Decker, and the notes left to him are weighing more heavily on his conscience as he now realizes that only he has the power to stop the murders.

He feels guilty for the murders that have been committed, and he feels premature guilt for the ones that he is sure are following. As human care for others begins to permeate Decker's existence, it seems obvious that his brain injury is not as pronounced as once thought, as he is regaining some compassion for others.

Important Terms/Characters:
Sandy – Lancaster's daughter, who has Down's syndrome
Earl – Lancaster's husband

Study Questions:
1. What is the significance of the crime scene at Lancaster's house?

25. Chapters 49-51

What Happens:
Decker returns to his hotel room, deciding that he will commit suicide like he had planned to do once his family was murdered. However, before he is able to do so, Captain Miller shows up and convinces him not to. He tells Decker that if he commits suicide, the killer has won and the force won't be able to track him or her down. He asks Decker to postpone killing himself, and instead, to join him at Lancaster's house to go over more clues.

When he gets there, Jamison is there. She has been called by Miller and requested to help find the killer. The duo arrives at the protective custody house where Lancaster is being kept. When they get there, Decker realizes that the Lancaster home was incredibly clean and asks Lancaster if they had a maid service. When she says that they did, Decker wonders if perhaps the maid is the killer. They call the maid company and find that a woman had called to cancel the appointment, yet a maid had showed up.

Decker realizes that the killer called to cancel he appointment, then used the standing date to insert he house and get a key. Decker continues to replay the image from the camera in his mind, finding it odd the way that the waitress had gotten in and out of the car. He borrows Bogart's jet, and he, Bogart, and Jamison fly to Chicago to meet with a doctor at the research institute. Decker asks Dr. Marshall about a patient at the time whose name was Belinda Wyatt. Belinda Wyatt was gang-raped at age 16.

While Dr. Marshall is skeptical to divulge any information, he eventually tells Decker that Belinda was a hermaphrodite and had two different sex organs. Dr. Marshall divulges that Sizemore and Belinda Wyatt had an affair. Decker asks if the doctor can help him get in touch with Belinda, but the doctor only has her parents' last known addresses. It is obvious that her parents did not have a good relationship with Belinda.

Analysis:
Decker's discovery of Belinda Wyatt's dual-gender is an important note, as it leads credence to the theory that the waitress could have been a man in drag. However, the new discovery of Belinda Wyatt doesn't answer all questions, as the reader still doesn't know how Decker dissed her or what the connection is between Belinda Wyatt and football.

The reader does, however, know that Wyatt's life is probably incredibly complicated—nearly as complicated as her genitalia. The comments by Dr. Marshall lead the reader to wonder what happened between Belinda and her parents, and leave some idea of what may have transpired. In addition, the knowledge of Belinda's dual-gender makes the reader start to feel sorry for the killer and allows the reader to see the killer in a more humane aspect.

Important Terms/Characters:
Dr. Marshall - Decker's doctor from the research institute
Belinda Wyatt – a woman at the research institute who was born with both male and female genitalia

Study Questions:
1. Describe Belinda Wyatt. How have her experiences affected her?

Interesting Quotes:
"It's a total package, particularly when one is dealing with the mind, so we needed to understand everything. And her parents had no objection. I think they wanted to wash their hands of it."

26. Chapters 52-53

What Happens:
Decker, Jamison and Bogart follow the address given to them to
Colorado in an effort to go see Belinda's parents. While they're
there, Bogart asks Decker why he suspects that Belinda is the
shooter, since she's a woman. Decker tells him that when Belinda
got in and out of the car, she did so in a very feminine way, by
covering herself with her hands. He claims only a person who was
raised as a girl would behave that way.

He believes that Belinda was probably seduced by Dr. Sizemore
while at the institute, which caused her to lash out. Decker can't
make the connection between Belinda and Leopold, however.
When they get to the parents' house in Colorado, they find that the
Denver federal agents and the local police are both there
investigating. Belinda's parents are both dead. When they are
there, Decker finds a box of letters that Belinda sent her parents
while at the institute.

On the back of each of the letters, there's one letter. When they put
them together, the letters make a threat to kill people. Bogart tells
reasons for killers to mutilate their victims' genitalia, even without
raping.

Analysis:
As the details of Belinda Wyatt's life come to the surface, it
becomes obvious that she is an incredibly troubled woman. Her
relationship with her parents, who practically disowned her
because of her condition, highlights her need for acceptance and
the pain that she felt as a result of her condition. This pain causes
the reader to feel sympathy for Belinda, opening a new conflict for
the reader as the reader has now recognized that Belinda is the
killer, and yet, the reader feels sorry for her. However, the link
between Belinda and Leopold still hasn't been established, and the
reader must still try to figure out what their connection is. Leopold,

as opposed to Belinda, has gained little to no sympathy from the reader at this point in the story.

Important Terms/Characters:
Lane and Ashby Wyatt – Belinda's parents, who are dead at the house

Study Questions:
1. What is the significance of the Wyatt's mansion? What is their relationship with their daughter like?

Interesting Quotes:
"Bogart looked at the person's hand. It was knifed into the narrow crevice between the thighs, edging the skirt down."

27. Chapters 54-56

What Happens:
Decker returns to his hotel room and begins to think about Belinda and Leopold. He wonders how they are connected, and begins to reminisce about his time at the institute. He wonders what he might have said or done to Belinda to make her upset. He switches tracks to thinking about Leopold, trying to place him and how he knows Belinda.

He realizes that Leopold may be European, due to his accent and a few of the words he has said during their interview. He asks Bogart to look into the international databases to try and find Leopold's real name and his background. Decker returns to the 7-Eleven where he originally thought he dissed the killer, finding that Billy, the boy that was working at the 7-Eleven is no longer employed there. He realizes that Billy was actually Belinda.

When he calls Bogart to tell him that Belinda is actually Billy, Bogart informs him that Leopold is from Austria and his entire family was murdered, though the killer was never found. Decker, Jamison, and Lancaster all meet in the library to look over more information that has to do with the case. Decker calls Dr.

Marshall to ask him for more information about Belinda's parents, and finds that Mr. and Mrs. Wyatt were afraid of Belinda because of the threats she made. He asks for their earlier address and finds that they lived in a modest neighborhood and moved into a mansion shortly after. He wonders how the Wyatt's got all of their money, since they weren't always rich.

Analysis:
Decker's memory allows him to form a new hunch that perhaps the Billy at the 7-Eleven was in fact Belinda. It is obvious that Belinda has learned to play both sides of her gender equally, as she was not only the waitress but also the boy in the 7-Eleven. As Decker

researches more into Wyatt's background, a new discrepancy comes up.

It seems odd that when the Wyatt's let go of Belinda, they acquired extra income. It is fishy, not only to the police force but also to the reader as the reader must wonder if the Wyatt's used their daughter for financial gain. In addition, Leopold's background is suspicious as the reader finds out that Leopold's family was murdered, but the murderer was never found. The reader has to wonder how Leopold knows Belinda, and how the murderers are connected.

Important Terms/Characters:
N/A

Study Questions:
1. Why is it important to note that Sebastian Leopold is from Europe? How did Decker realize that he was not from America?

Interesting Quotes:

"I don't hate the world," said Decker. "I only hate some of the people who unfortunately live in it."

28. Chapters 57-59

What Happens:
Decker realizes that Belinda's brain condition was a result of her violent rape. As he meets with Lancaster, Bogart, and Jamison, they go over the Wyatt's finances and find that the couple was given a large amount of money from an unknown source. He wonders if perhaps Belinda's attackers paid them off.

The crew decides they should go to Belinda's hometown to find out more information about her rape and the attackers. When they get to Utah, they find out that Belinda's childhood home was bought just before Decker's family was murdered, and Decker wonders if Belinda might have bought it herself. They search the house and find a newspaper article about a cop who went missing named Giles Evers. Decker believes that Evers was probably one of Belinda's attackers, and also that she probably exacted revenge on him. He thinks that maybe all of her attackers were police officers and that Giles father paid the Wyatt's to be quiet about it.

Decker suggests they go to Giles' father Clyde's house. When they get there, they find that he is poor and the Wyatt's have taken all of his money. While he doesn't want to talk about it, the crew convinces him to and he tells them that the rape was performed by football players, a football coach, an assistant principal, and his son, a police officer. Decker realizes that Belinda killed the same number of people in the same positions at Mansfield, and that Decker represents the police officer.

In addition, he tells them about an article he received in the mail from an organization called Justice Denied, about police officers who had committed heinous crimes and gotten away with them. Leopold's wife and daughter are on the list of those murdered, connecting him with Belinda.

Analysis:

As more of Belinda's story is revealed, the reader's sympathy for her grows and the reader must decide where loyalties lie. Belinda's life, ruined by not only her condition but her brutal rape, was only made worse by her parents' reluctance to bring justice to her life. Instead, her parents furthered her hatred by betraying her. Their lack of love and affection for their daughter is highlighted by their ability to be bought by Giles' father.

In addition, the group of men that raped Belinda prove to be similar to the group she murdered, a distinction that is not lost on the reader. Belinda is exacting revenge on her rapists by killing those similar to them, however, it is still unclear as to why she has targeted this specific group that is connected to Decker. Leopold's involvement with Justice Denied makes the reader wonder what his life is like and why he and Belinda have gotten together. The reader begins to feel sympathy for Leopold, as well, as he has been in a similar boat as Belinda.

Important Terms/Characters:
Giles Evers – one of Belinda's rapists, who disappeared. He was a cop.
Clyde Evers – Giles father, who paid off the Wyatt's to keep quiet.
Justice Denied – an organization about police officers who commit heinous crimes
Caroline and Deidre Leopold – Sebastian's family, who was murdered

Study Questions:
1. How is Belinda's rape related to the school shooting at Mansfield High School?

Interesting Quotes:
"They were bound by their conditions. They were connected by their histories, their paths crossing at a traumatic point in their lives."

29. Chapters 60-62

What Happens:
As the crew looks over the case of Leopold's wife and daughter's murders, they are unable to find any evidence that a police officer committed the crimes against them. They also can't figure out why Belinda has targeted him. He gets Miller's permission to look through the evidence files on the cases, and as he looks through the uniform and badge taken in police custody from Lafferty's murder, he sees the X on his badge.

He remembers suddenly that years ago, he told the group at the research institute about his plans to become a police officer. He realizes that Belinda felt personally slighted by the football player who turned into a police officer. He finds that the Wyatt's money has been disappearing each month, and believes that the money is going to the Justice Denied organization. When he looks into the organization, he realizes that Belinda and Leopold are on the other end of the website. He decides he will meet with them and allow them to kill him.

He follows their instructions, going through a series of different steps before he is finally in the car with Billy and Sebastian, who holds him at gunpoint. Decker talks more with Belinda and finds out more information about her life and the murders.

Analysis:
Decker's decision to offer himself up to Belinda and Sebastian showcases a new depth of human care and understanding that he had been previously missing. While Decker did not value his own life throughout the novel, finding that suicide would be a good option, Decker's current situation is much more favorable as it could lead to the saving of future lives.

His realization that he slighted Belinda by telling the group he would be a police officer highlights Belinda's mental illness and shows that she is a woman who was deeply troubled, as it is obvious to the reader that this was in no way directed at her. She chose symbolism over literalism when exacting her revenge, choosing to hurt more people than just the ones who had hurt her. Her desire to be a male, rather than a female, showcases that she feels like a victim and does not want to be in the same position that she was as a teenager.

However, she is unable to function in society as a "normal" male, and must resort to a similar level of brutality that the males in her own life exerted over her. Her rape, plus the lack of affection from her father, removed any sort of human kindness from the male sex in Belinda's eyes, and she is unable to see men as anything other than predators. Now, with that example and her desire to not become the prey, she has become the predator herself.

Important Terms/Characters:
N/A

Study Questions:
1. What did Decker do that caused Belinda to want to exact revenge on him? Was she right to do so? Why or why not?

Interesting Quotes:
"There was no remorse. There was nothing behind the eyes. She was thirty-six now. And he doubted she had had an easy, normal day in the last thirty of them. That couldn't help but change you. How could you respect or appreciate or care about a world and the people in that world when they loathed the fact that you shared their planet?"

"Men are predators. Women are their prey. I chose never to be the prey again. I chose to be the predator."

30. Chapter 63-65

What Happens:
Belinda and Leopold tie Decker to a chair, and Decker, knowing
that murderers like to tell how they performed their deeds, asks
them to give him more information about the case. As they talk,
Decker reinvents the story, painting Leopold as a scam artist.
When he does so, Leopold stabs him in the leg and smacks his
head, however, the seed of doubt has already been planted in
Belinda's mind about Leopold's intentions.

Leopold admits that he murdered his own family, and Belinda feels
betrayed. Decker uses the moment where Leopold turns to Belinda
to confess to crash into Leopold. Decker knocks Leopold to the
ground and suffocates him under his body weight. Belinda dies as
a result of Leopold's shot, and Decker watches her die. Decker
leaves the scene and drives Belinda's van away from the scene and
calls Bogart.

Decker goes to the hospital to be checked for injuries. While there,
he finds out that Clyde Evers received a package with Giles
severed head inside of it, from Belinda. Bogart invites Decker to
work with him and the FBI, along with Jamison. Decker and
Jamison both decide to accept the offer and move to D.C.

Analysis:
After solving the murder of his family, Decker is finally able to
close his eyes and relax without seeing blue or dancing threes
everywhere he goes. The revelation that Leopold was the
ringmaster behind the whole plan and that he was just a murderer,
not a bereaved father, gives more credence to the idea that
sympathy should be felt for Belinda.

As Belinda tells more of her story, the reader's sympathy grows to
the point where the reader truly doesn't want Belinda to go through
any more pain. It seems obvious that she has had an unfair life, and

natural sympathy makes the reader want her to have the chance to experience a better one. However, this is not the case.

Decker, surprisingly, shares this sympathy and seems to feel protective in some ways over Belinda, a feeling he had previously only had for his wife and daughter. The addition of Jamison and Decker to the FBI is an interesting one and further sets up the possibility for the two to work together.

Important Terms/Characters:
N/A

Study Questions:
1. How does Decker kill Leopold? Were you expecting this turn of events? Why or why not?
2. How has this case given Decker a reason to live? What good came out of it?

Interesting Quotes:
"Amos Decker closed his eyes.
And with it his mind.
If only for a little while.
For just a little while."

31. Critical Reviews:

Most reviews of David Baldacci's "The Memory Man" are positive. Many reviewers compliment Baldacci's writing style and his ability to bring humor into a thriller. While most of Baldacci's novels feature a protagonist who has the physical build of a police officer or another investigator, the protagonist of "The Memory Man" is somewhat deformed and unattractive. In addition, his mannerisms are difficult for the reader to root for. However, the inclusion of his brain trauma and his synesthesia and hyperthymesia make him more lovable and endearing than he otherwise would be.

Many critics, also, highlight Baldacci's plot. The story, which is somewhat slow-moving in the first few chapters, picks up pace significantly after the groundwork has been laid to explain Decker's personality. However, many critics have noted the somewhat implausible storyline. These critics have found that the storyline seemed a bit convoluted to make sense. In addition, the background of the killer seemed too improbable to be realistic. However, for most critics, this did not diminish the enjoyment of the novel.

Overall, critics are mostly positive on "The Memory Man" and state that the benefits of the novel far outweigh any negatives.

32. Final Thoughts:

I really enjoyed David Baldacci's "The Memory Man". I thought that the storyline of the novel, which intertwines hot button topics like police brutality, intersex conditions, and school shootings was incredibly well done. The addition of Decker's conditions of hyperthymesia and synesthesia were fascinating, and made him a more well-rounded character than he would have otherwise been. I found these two conditions to be interesting, particularly coupled with his job as a detective. The character of Amos Decker was incredibly complex, and throughout the novel, I found myself wanting to know more about him and his brain injury.

The pace of the novel was perfect for me, as I enjoyed learning about Decker in the first few chapters, and then as the story progressed, I found myself wanting to read more and more. I found that when each chapter concluded, I was anxious to read another one. The twists and turns were unexpected, but unlike many reviewers, I didn't find them impossible or implausible. I enjoyed following the twists of Decker's life, and trying to figure out the mysteries as he did. While most of the time I was not ahead of Decker, there were a few times where I figured something out ahead of him.

One of my favorite parts of the novel, however, was the psychological reactions of the killer, Belinda Wyatt. I found her condition of hermaphroditism coupled with her memory incredibly fascinating. In addition, I thought her childhood was extremely interesting and added a lot of understanding to her character. While at the beginning of the novel, I hated the killer and thought of her as vicious and sadistic, by the end of the novel, after learning more about Belinda's past, I started to feel more compassion for her. At the very end of the novel, I actually was rooting for Belinda to be free rather than to have to pay for her crimes. To me, that is the mark of a good author.

I have never read a novel by Baldacci before this one, but after reading "The Memory Man", I want to read many more.

33. Glossary:

Amos Decker – a police investigator whose family was murdered a year and a half earlier; he now has synesthesia and an above-average memory.

Cassandra Decker – Amos's wife, a murder victim

Molly Decker – Amos's 9 year old daughter, a murder victim

Johnny Sacks – Amos's brother-in-law, a murder victim

Residence Inn – the motel where Amos lives after he gets off the street

Slick – a con-man that Amos Decker is hired to bust

Jenny Marks - the woman that Slick is seeing, who is rich off Daddy's money.

Hyperthymesia – a condition Decker has where a person's memory is exceptional and has no faults

Synesthesia – a condition Decker has where two senses are connected

Mary Lancaster –Decker's old partner, who is still a member of the police force

Sebastian Leopold – the man who turned himself in for the murders of three of Decker's family

Dwayne LeCroix – a football player who hit Decker so hard he had a brain injury

Alexandra Jamison – a reporter who wants to interview Decker

7 – Eleven – the place where Leopold apparently met Decker which caused him to want to murder the family

Sally Brimmer – a woman at the police precinct who shows Decker to Leopold's cell

Pete Rourke – a man on the police force

Mansfield High – the high school where there was a shooting

Captain Mackenzie Miller – the captain of the police force who shows up at Decker's hotel

Debbie Watson – the first person to be murdered in the school shooting, a high school senior

Melissa Dalton – a student who gave a testimony about a loud vacuum sound an hour before the shooting began

Sheila Lynch – the prosecuting attorney for the case against Sebastian Leopold

Billy – an employee at the 7-Eleven

George Watson – Debbie's father

Beth Watson – Debbie's mother

Simon Watson – George's grandfather, who worked at the army base before he passed away

Special Agent Ross Bogart – An FBI agent sent from Washington DC to help investigate the school shooting

Special Agent Lafferty – Ross Bogart's assistant who takes notes

McDonald Army Base – the army base that is shut down but located near the school

Mallard 2000 – the email address of the killer, referring to Duckton Avenue in Chicago

Chris Sizemore – a psychologist of the Cognitive Research Institute who disliked Decker

Dr. Rabinowitz – one of the research doctors from the Cognitive Research Institute

Cognitive Research Institute – the research institute where Decker attended after his brain injury

Daisy – the owner of the flower shop in the same building that the Cognitive Research Institute used to be located in

Sandy – Lancaster's daughter, who has Down's syndrome

Earl – Lancaster's husband

Dr. Marshall - Decker's doctor from the research institute

Belinda Wyatt – a woman at the research institute who was born with both male and female genitalia

Lane and Ashby Wyatt – Belinda's parents, who are dead at the house

Giles Evers – one of Belinda's rapists, who disappeared. He was a cop.

Clyde Evers – Giles father, who paid off the Wyatt's to keep quiet.

Justice Denied – an organization about police officers who commit heinous crimes

Caroline and Deidre Leopold – Sebastian's family, who was murdered

34. Recommended Reading:

"The Innocent" – David Baldacci
"President's Shadow" – Brad Meltzer
"The English Spy" – Daniel Silva
"Gathering Prey" – John Sandford
"All the Light We Cannot See" - Anthony Doerr

Printed in the USA
CPSIA information can be obtained
at www.ICGtesting.com
LVHW011915060624
782552LV00005B/225